SECRET AGENT

JACK STALWART

The Mystery
of the
Mona Lisa:
FRANCE

Join Secret Agent Jack Stalwart

on his other adventures:

The Escape of the Deadly Dinosaur: **USA**

The Search for the Sunken Treasure: **AUSTRALIA**

The Secret of the Sacred Temple: **CAMBODIA**

The Mystery
of the
Mona Lisa:
FRANCE

Elizabeth Singer Hunt

Illustrated by Brian Williamson

RED FOX

THE MYSTERY OF THE MONA LISA: FRANCE
A RED FOX BOOK 978 1 862 30297 6

First published in Great Britain by Chubby Cheeks Publications Limited
Published in this edition by Red Fox,
an imprint of Random House Children's Books

Chubby Cheeks edition published 2004
This edition published 2006

The Random House Group Limited makes every effort to ensure that the papers used in its
books are made from trees that have been legally sourced from well-managed and credibly
certified forests. Our paper procurement policy can be found at:
www.randomhouse.co.uk/paper.htm

Set in Meta, Trixie, American Typewriter, Luggagetag, Gill Sans Condensed and Serpentine.

Red Fox Books are published by Random House Children's Books,
61–63 Uxbridge Road, London W5 5SA.
A Random House Group Company

www.**kids**at**randomhouse**.co.uk

Addresses for companies within The Random House Group Limited can be found at:
www.randomhouse.co.uk/offices.htm

THE RANDOM HOUSE GROUP Limited Reg. No. 954009

A CIP catalogue record for this book is available from the British Library.

Printed and bound in Great Britain by Cox & Wyman Ltd, Reading, Berkshire

For Andy, Morgan and Corinne

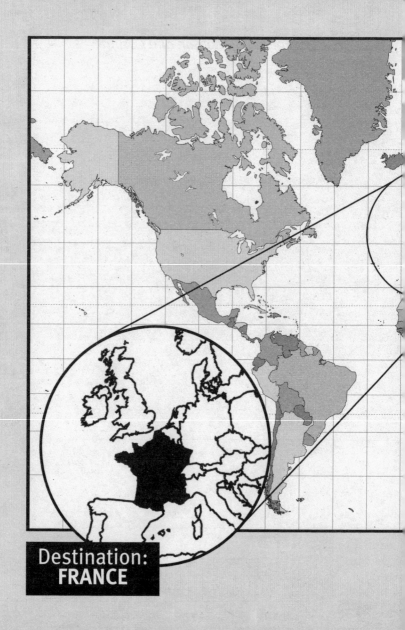

Destination:
FRANCE

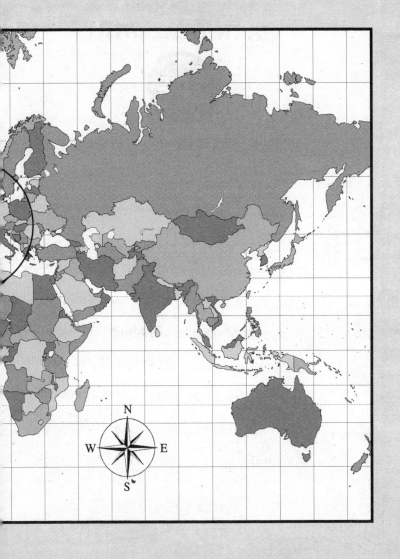

My name is Jack Stalwart. My older brother,

Max, was a secret agent for you, until he

disappeared on one of your missions. Now I

want to be a secret agent too. If you choose

me, I will be an excellent secret agent and get

rid of evil villains, just like my brother did.

Sincerely,

Jack Stalwart

THINGS YOU'LL FIND IN EVERY BOOK

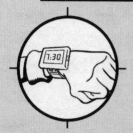

Watch Phone: The only gadget Jack wears all the time, even when he's not on official business. His Watch Phone is the central gadget that makes most others work. There are lots of important features, most importantly the 'C' button, which reveals the code of the day – necessary to unlock Jack's Secret Agent Book Bag. There are buttons on both sides, one of which ejects his life-saving Melting Ink Pen. Beyond these functions, it also works as a phone and, of course, gives Jack the time of day.

Global Protection Force (GPF): The GPF is the organization Jack works for. It's a worldwide force of young secret agents whose aim is to protect the world's people, places and possessions. No one knows exactly where its main offices are located (all correspondence and gadgets for repair are sent to a special PO Box, and training is held at various locations around the world), but Jack thinks it's somewhere cold, like the Arctic Circle.

Whizzy: Jack's magical miniature globe. Almost every night at precisely 7:30 p.m., the GPF uses Whizzy to send Jack the identity of the country that he must travel to. Whizzy can't talk, but he can cough up messages. Jack's parents don't know Whizzy is anything more than a normal globe.

The Magic Map: The magical map hanging on Jack's bedroom wall. Unlike most maps, the GPF's map is made of a mysterious wood. Once Jack inserts the country piece from Whizzy, the map swallows Jack whole and sends him away on his missions. When he returns, he arrives precisely one minute after he left.

Secret Agent Book Bag: The Book Bag that Jack wears on every adventure. Licensed only to GPF secret agents, it contains top-secret gadgets necessary to foil bad guys and escape certain death. To activate the bag before each mission, Jack must punch in a secret code given to him by his Watch Phone. Once he's away, all he has to do is place his finger on the zip, which identifies him as the owner of the bag and immediately opens.

THE STALWART FAMILY

Jack's dad, John

He moved the family to England when Jack was two, in order to take a job with an aerospace company. As far as Jack knows, his dad designs and manufactures aeroplane parts. Jack's dad thinks he is an ordinary boy and that his other son, Max, attends a school in Switzerland. Jack's dad is American and his mum is British, which makes Jack a bit of both.

Jack's mum, Corinne

One of the greatest mums as far as Jack is concerned. When she and her husband received a letter from a posh school in Switzerland inviting Max to attend, they were overjoyed. Since Max left six months ago, they have received numerous notes in Max's handwriting telling them he's OK. Little do they know it's all a lie and that it's the GPF sending those letters.

Jack's older brother, Max

Two years ago, at the age of nine, Max joined the GPF. Max used to tell Jack about his adventures and show him how to work his secret-agent gadgets. When the family received a letter inviting Max to attend a school in Europe, Jack figured it was to do with the GPF. Max told him he was right, but that he couldn't tell Jack anything about why he was going away.

Nine-year-old Jack Stalwart

Four months ago, Jack received an anonymous note saying: 'Your brother is in danger. Only you can save him.' As soon as he could, Jack applied to be a secret agent too. Since that time, he's battled some of the world's most dangerous villains, and hopes some day in his travels to find and rescue his brother, Max.

DESTINATION:
France

France is located on the continent of Europe

•

Paris is the capital city of France

•

Almost nine million people live in this city

•

One of the world's most famous museums, the Louvre, is located in Paris

•

France is a member of the European Union and its currency is the euro

French people love eating interesting food, including snails, which are called *escargot* (pronounced *s-car-go*) in French

•

The Eiffel Tower, one of the most famous landmarks in Paris, is 320 metres tall and was the tallest structure in the world until 1931

•

The English Channel is a narrow sea that separates the north of France from the United Kingdom

MONA LISA:
Facts and Figures

The *Mona Lisa* was painted by Leonardo da Vinci and is one of the most famous paintings in the world

●

It was probably painted between 1503 and 1506

●

Originally the painting was larger than today, but at some point the sides were cut off

●

Each year millions of people visit the Louvre museum in Paris where is it on display

On Monday August 21, 1911, the *Mona Lisa* was actually stolen from the Louvre by a man named Vincenzo Perugia. It took the police over two years to find it

●

The painting measures just 53 x 76 centimetres and is hung behind unbreakable glass to protect it

PLACES IN PARIS

Arc de Triomphe (pronounced *Ark da Tree-omf*)

Champs Elysées (pronounced *Shoms El-ee-zay*)

The Eiffel Tower (pronounced *I-fill*)

Musée du Louvre (pronounced *Mew-say do Loo-vre*)

Musée de l'Homme (pronounced *Mew-say de lom*)

Musée d'Orsay (pronounced *Mew-say Dor-say*)

Place de la Concorde
(pronounced *Plass de la Con-cord*)

Pompidou (pronounced *Pom-pee-do*)

River Seine (pronounced *Sane*)

Tuileries gardens (pronounced *Too-i-ler-ee*)

SECRET AGENT GADGET INSTRUCTION MANUAL

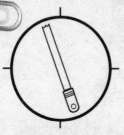

Magic Key Maker: One of the most useful gadgets in the GPF arsenal. It's perfect when you don't have a key to open a lock. Just insert this long, rubber stick into a keyhole or ignition and watch as it melts and oozes inside. Wait a few seconds for it to harden into a key, and then use it to gain access to whatever you need.

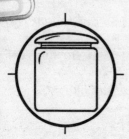

Time-Release Vapours:

Whenever another secret agent or trusted contact has been knocked out, use the Time-Release Vapours to bring them back to consciousness. Just open the tub, place a small amount of the cream on your finger and rub it under their nose. The vapours should work to wake them within minutes.

The Hypno-Disc: One of the most useful gadgets available to GPF secret agents today. The Hypno-Disc has two functions:

1) to hypnotize your opponent and
2) to save you from deadly force

fields (lasers, hypnotizing lights, etc.). To activate, turn the dial on the back of this circular disc in a clockwise direction. The disc will spin, throwing out a hypnotic light that will transfix your opponent. To save yourself from force fields coming your way, turn the dial on the back in an anti-clockwise direction. The spinning will reverse, sucking any deadly light into the device and trapping it there.

Chapter 1:
The Vanishing Lady

The museum in Paris had been closed for several hours and the Bon Homme cleaning crew were busy at work. Over a hundred cleaners were scurrying through the huge museum, mopping the floors and dusting the railings, taking care not to damage the precious paintings that hung on its walls.

One of the rooms in the museum was known as the '*Mona Lisa* room', because on a special fake wall in the middle hung the most famous painting in the world.

1

The *Mona Lisa* was a painting of a woman clothed in a brown dress with a mysterious smile on her face. It was painted over four hundred years ago by an artist named Leonardo da Vinci. It was so valuable that the museum had invested in a bullet-proof-glass security box, which was fixed over the painting to protect it from anyone who wanted to do it harm.

On this night, Hélène, one of Bon Homme's senior cleaners, made her way to the *Mona Lisa* room. As usual, she entered the room after her assistant, Jean Paul, had mopped the floor. She walked over to the glass box with the *Mona Lisa* inside and pulled out a special dusting cloth. She lifted the cloth and tried to wipe over it. But something was wrong. The front of the box was no longer there.

Hélène blinked twice and then let out a

piercing scream that shook the entire room. 'The *Mona Lisa* is gone!' she screamed. 'The world's most famous painting has been stolen from the Louvre!'

Chapter 2:
The Magic Map

In a different country, nine-year-old Secret
Agent Jack Stalwart was sitting in his
bedroom at his desk doing his homework.
His Year 5 art teacher, Mr Yates, had
asked the class to draw a picture of their
favourite comic-book hero by the next
day. Jack's choice, Super Smash, was one
of four superheroes who lived on the
planet Green and battled with the likes
of Tortua, the nastiest female villain ever
seen. Jack loved reading about Super
Smash's adventures and was thinking

about doing just that when there was a knock from inside his right-hand desk drawer.

Drat, thought Jack. He knew what that meant. He looked at his Watch Phone. It was 7:00 p.m. He carefully opened the drawer and peeked inside. There, lying in his desk, was a new DVD. The GPF often snuck things like that into Jack's room as a way to prepare him for his upcoming missions. This DVD was entitled: *Da Vinci's Masterpiece: The Mona Lisa*.

He carried it over to the TV in the corner of his room and put it into the built-in DVD player. Almost instantly, a programme on the history of the famous

5

painting began. What Jack didn't know, the DVD told him, so that by the time it was finished he was fully informed. He looked at his Watch Phone as the credits rolled. It was 7:30 p.m.

Just as he expected, a familiar whirring sound came from the other corner of his room. His trusty miniature globe, Whizzy, was starting to spin. Jack rushed over to Whizzy. By now the globe was spinning so hard that he had smoke coming out of his ears.

'Come on, Whizzy!' Jack cheered. 'I know you can do it.'

'Ahem!' coughed Whizzy, and out of his mouth popped a jigsaw piece in the

shape of an unknown country. It landed
on the floor next to Jack's foot. Whizzy let
out a big whoosh as he settled down
again.

'This one is quite large,' commented
Jack as he picked up the piece. 'And after
seeing that DVD, I bet I know where I'm
going tonight.'

Jack carried the piece over to the far side
of his bedroom, to the large map of the
world that was hanging on his wall. It
looked just like an ordinary map, but in
fact it was a Magic Map from the GPF. It
transported him around the world to battle
evil villains and bring them to justice.

He lifted the piece and placed it over
the map. He steered it towards the centre
of Europe and instantly the jigsaw slotted
in. Jack stepped back to take a look. The
name 'FRANCE' appeared, then quickly
vanished.

'France!' said Jack. 'I knew it had to be France! I can't wait to go.'

Jack tapped the 'C' button on his Watch Phone. Instantly the code of the day was displayed across its screen. He dashed over to his bed and knelt down next to it, pulling his Book Bag out from underneath. He punched in the code on its lock – C-H-E-E-S-E – and unzipped the bag, looking inside. He had to make sure that all of his secret-agent gadgets were there before he left.

Magic Key Maker. Check. Magic Steps. Check. Melting Ink Pen. Check. Jack closed the bag and turned to Whizzy. 'I think I'm ready to go,' he said.

Jack raced back to the wall just as a warm yellow light was beginning to glow inside the country of France. The beam continued to grow until all of Jack's room was filled with brightness.

'Off to France!' Jack cried. And with those words, the yellow light burst and swallowed Jack into the Magic Map.

Chapter 3:
The Glass Museum

When Jack arrived he noticed two things. The first was that it was morning and the second was that he was standing in the middle of a large pyramid with a glass ceiling. For a moment he wondered whether the map had thrown him off course.

'Am I in Egypt?' he wondered out loud.

'No. I can assure you that you are not in Egypt,' a voice said from behind. 'You are in Paris, the capital city of France. I am Chief Inspector Henri Pierre. You must be

Jack,' he said, extending his hand. 'The Global Protection Force said that they would be sending their finest.'

Chief Inspector Henri Pierre was a large man with a big belly, who looked as if he had enjoyed too many puddings. When he smiled his eyes twinkled and his moustache wriggled. Although Henri Pierre was losing his hair, he still looked very young to be a chief inspector.

'Nice to meet you, Chief Inspector,' said Jack, showing his GPF badge.

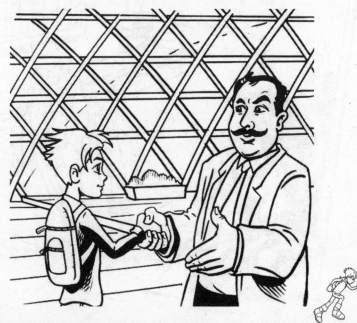

'You can call me Henri,' said the chief inspector.

'Well then, Henri, what seems to be the problem?' Jack asked, eager to find out about his next mission.

'You are standing in the middle of the Louvre, one of the world's greatest museums,' explained Henri. 'Inside here are some of the rarest and most

expensive pieces of art. Last night, one of our most precious paintings, the *Mona Lisa*, was stolen right from under our noses. We think it happened sometime between closing time at 6:00 p.m., and 8:00 p.m., when one of the cleaners noticed that it was missing.'

'I don't understand,' said Jack. 'Didn't your video surveillance equipment record the thief in action?'

'No, it didn't,' answered Henri. 'It is most strange – there is no record of anyone going in or out of the room before the cleaners,' he added. 'That is why we called the GPF. We need your special skills to find the *Mona Lisa* and make sense of this horrible mess.'

'No problem, Henri,' said Jack. 'I'm sure I can find the *Mona Lisa* and return it to the museum. First I'd like to see the room where the painting was stolen from. Then I'd like to meet the cleaner who discovered that it was missing. He or she might be able to provide some clues that could help in the investigation.'

'I agree,' said the chief inspector. 'First things first,' he went on. 'Let me show you to the *Mona Lisa* room.'

Chapter 4: The Investigation

Jack followed Henri through the halls of the museum past some of the most amazing works of art that Jack had ever seen. Beyond the *Mona Lisa* painting, Jack knew that the Louvre was famous for containing art from Ancient Egypt and Greece.

Mr Yates often talked about the Louvre museum and even promised to take Jack's class on a field trip there one day. Jack passed through a room filled with sculptures of men, then came upon a room with a lone wall in the middle.

Henri pointed up ahead. 'That's where the lady of the museum used to hang,' he said, referring to the *Mona Lisa*. 'You can see the thief was able not only to get past our security systems but also to cut off the front of the bullet-proof-glass box that helped protect her.'

Jack walked over to the wall and looked up at what was left. There was a hook where the painting had hung and the remains of the outer box. What was strange to Jack was that whatever had sawn through the box had done it so that the cut was nice and flat. Normally, Jack reasoned, when glass was broken there were jags or breaks in the glass left behind. But when Jack ran his finger over its edge, the glass was perfectly smooth.

'The only thing I know that can cut this finely,' said Jack to Henri, 'is a laser.'

'A laser, you say,' said Henri, somewhat surprised. 'That's an interesting observation.'

'And as far as I can tell there don't seem to be any pieces of laser equipment left behind,' said Jack as he looked around the room. 'What about fingerprints?' he continued, carrying on with questions related to his investigation.

'We've already dusted,' said the chief inspector. 'I sent a team in as soon as the *Mona Lisa* was discovered missing. They scoured the walls, railings and, of course, the glass box itself. When I got word that you were on your way, I told the team to clear out until you were finished. The only part of the room they didn't get to examine was the floor.'

Jack got down on his hands and knees and looked across the floor of the great room for any clues. Just ahead of him, he spied a single strand of hair. It was such a distinctive shade of red, he couldn't help but notice it. He picked it up and examined it closely.

Knowing that Inspector Pierre's team had been all over the place dusting for fingerprints, he turned to Henri.

'Does anyone in your team have red hair like this one?' he asked, showing the strand to Henri. He was trying to eliminate one of the chief inspector's officers as the one who'd left the hair.

'No,' replied Henri. 'No one has red hair like that.'

Given what Henri had just said, Jack figured it had been left by either the last cleaner to leave the room or by the crook.

Jack crouched down to his knees and opened his Book Bag. Inside was a clear, square box with a silver digital display on the outside. This was the GPF's DNA

Decoder. Since everyone in the world has a different DNA – or part of the cells that tells our bodies what to do and what to look like – the GPF developed the DNA Decoder. It could take something as simple as a hair, and tell a secret agent who it belonged to.

'Do you mind if I analyse this?' asked Jack, referring to the strand of hair.

'Not at all,' said the chief inspector. 'Be my guest.'

Jack took the DNA Decoder out and opened it up, placing the single strand of hair inside. He closed it and pushed the 'decode' button. Instantly the results were displayed: UNKNOWN.

Great, thought Jack, shaking his head in frustration. If this was the hair of the crook, Jack figured he or she was a first-timer.

'Well,' said Jack, standing up and gathering his evidence and his bag, 'I think it's time I met the cleaner.'

'Certainly,' said Henri. 'The person you need to speak to is Hélène. She's sitting downstairs waiting to be interviewed. I'll show you the way.'

Chapter 5:
The Interview

Jack followed Henri down two floors to a
small room on the lower level. Waiting
for him was a woman with brown hair
dressed in a blue-and-white-striped
cleaner's uniform. She was sitting on a
chair beside a desk. As far as Jack could
tell she looked like an honest woman,
although Jack knew you could never be
sure. She seemed to be terribly upset by
the whole thing as she was crying a lot
and spent most of her time wiping the
tears away from her eyes.

'*Bonjour*,' said Jack as he closed the

door behind him. *'Je m'appelle Jack Stalwart.'*

'Hello,' replied the woman. She could tell that Jack wasn't from France, so she spoke to him in English. 'My name is Hélène,' she said.

'I am here from the Global Protection Force,' Jack explained. 'I'm trying to figure out who took the *Mona Lisa*. As you know, this is a very serious crime and therefore everyone involved is a suspect,' he said.

Hélène wiped her tears away again and looked across at him with scared eyes.

'Can you tell me,' he asked, 'what you were doing when you noticed the painting was missing and exactly what you saw?'

Hélène thought for a moment. 'Well,' she said, 'as I told Chief Inspector Pierre, I was on my way into the *Mona Lisa* room when my assistant, Jean Paul, rushed out.

I didn't think that much of it at the time, because Jean Paul is a bit of a nervous person. But then,' she added, 'I walked into the room and up to the box to clean the case and then I noticed it wasn't there.'

'What wasn't there?' asked Jack, making sure he understood her story.

'The *Mona Lisa*,' she said. 'And the box too. Well, at least the front of it.'

'Did you touch anything?' he asked.

'No,' she said. 'I left immediately and reported the theft to security.'

'What about Jean Paul?' said Jack. 'Did he say anything to you?' By now, Jack was thinking that perhaps Jean Paul had something to do with the crime.

'Not a thing,' she said, sniffing and wiping her eyes.

'What colour hair does Jean Paul have?' asked Jack.

'Brown,' said Hélène. 'Although sometimes in the light,' she added, 'it can look a bit red.'

Interesting, thought Jack as he and Henri looked at each other. He wondered if the hair he had found belonged to Jean Paul.

'It sounds as if I need to speak with Jean Paul,' said Jack. He'd pretty much ruled out Hélène as a suspect. 'Do you know where he lives?' he asked.

'He lives near the Eiffel Tower on Rue St Charles,' offered Hélène. 'In the house to the right of the barber shop.'

'Thanks,' said Jack. 'In the meantime,' he suggested, 'call Chief Inspector Pierre if you think of anything else.'

Hélène nodded and left the room, still sniffing back tears.

Jack rifled through his pocket and pulled out his secret-agent map of Paris. The Eiffel Tower and Rue St Charles weren't far from the Louvre.

'Rue St Charles, here I come,' he said to himself as he walked towards the door. 'Let's see if this Jean Paul can add anything else to the clues of this crime.'

Chapter 6:
The Chase

When Jack walked out of the great doors
of the Louvre, he found himself in the
middle of a square with a giant fountain
and lots of pretty flowers. In the distance,
he could see people lounging in chairs
near a water feature and a collection of
beautiful trees and shrubs. He looked at
his map. It looked as if he was facing a
garden called the Tuileries.

He turned left through the Tuileries and
headed towards a river called the Seine.
The mighty Seine flowed right through the

city of Paris, according to Jack's city map. He crossed over a bridge and turned right, following the Seine as it wound its way around. Up ahead he could see the Eiffel Tower, a massive iron monument that soared up into the sky and had an aerial on top that sent signals across the country.

Jack passed the Eiffel Tower and headed down Rue St Charles. The barber shop Hélène mentioned was on the corner.

When he reached the house, he stopped and knocked on the door.

There was no answer. He knocked again, this time a bit harder.

'*Bonjour*,' said a shy male voice from the other side.

'*Bonjour*,' said Jack. 'My name is Jack Stalwart and I am here to see Jean Paul. Is he in?'

All of a sudden Jack heard a clang and the sound of feet running away from the door. He heard a thud and then there was silence.

Jack called out. 'Jean Paul, is that you? Are you OK?' Still there was no answer.

Quickly, Jack tried to open the door. He was in luck – it was unlocked. He stepped inside and looked around. From an open window to his right, he could hear footsteps running down the street. He dashed to the window and looked outside.

'Jean Paul!' Jack yelled to the man who was running away. From what Jack could see, the man had reddish-brown hair. 'I just want to ask you a few questions!'

But the man kept running. Jack raced back to the front door and out onto the street, then started running in the same direction.

The man was running so fast and with such big strides, it was hard for Jack to keep up. He chased him as he raced past the Eiffel Tower and across a bridge. After that, the man headed towards the Place de la Concorde and turned right down a small road. He dashed past the post office, a supermarket and a bakery and down another street to the right.

'Wait!' Jack gasped. 'I just want to talk to you!'

Eventually the road that the man was running along ended and he was trapped with nowhere else to go. He turned to Jack with fear in his eyes.

'I didn't do it! I didn't do it!' he said, panting and trying to catch his breath.

'What do you mean?' asked Jack.

'I didn't steal the *Mona Lisa*,' said the man.

'Then why are you running away if you didn't do it?' asked Jack, still blocking his way.

'Because I saw something,' the man said, gasping for breath, 'and I am afraid. I am afraid for my life.'

Chapter 7:
The Confession

'It's OK,' said Jack, trying to calm him down. 'Maybe if you tell me what you saw I can help.' Jack wasn't entirely sure whether to trust Jean Paul, but for the moment he figured he'd give him a chance to explain.

The man plonked himself down on a dirty bench next to a rubbish skip and slumped over with his face in his hands.

'My name *is* Jean Paul,' he said, looking up at Jack. 'I work for Bon Homme Cleaners. I am Hélène's assistant. We are in charge of the *Mona Lisa* room.

'Last night,' explained Jean Paul, 'I was doing what I normally do – mopping the floors outside the *Mona Lisa* room. After I finished, I stepped in to mop the room itself. As I walked in, I saw a man standing in front of the *Mona Lisa*. His back was turned to me, so he didn't see me enter. I stepped back outside, but I peered round the corner to see what he was doing.

'You see,' Jean Paul added, 'Hélène and I are the only ones allowed in the room after the museum closes and I thought it was strange that he was in there.' He carried on, 'He put a black glove on his right hand. Then, out of nowhere, five thin red lights shot from his fingertips! He moved his hand around the edges of the box that protected the *Mona Lisa* and the lights sliced the front off as if it was a

soft cheese! I was so scared that I ran
away, past Hélène and out of the
museum.' Jack thought Jean Paul's
description was interesting, as he'd
already guessed that it was a laser that
had cut the glass. Maybe he was telling
the truth.

'Why didn't you tell someone?' asked
Jack.

'I was scared.' Jean Paul sighed.
'I thought no one would believe
me. And even if they did,

I didn't want the person who did this to know I was the one who saw him. He might come after me.'

'Can you tell me anything about the man himself?' asked Jack. 'What was he wearing?'

'He was dressed in black,' answered Jean Paul. 'His trousers were black, his shirt was black and his shoes were black. I couldn't see his face, because his back was towards me, but I could see that his hair was the colour of fire.'

'He had red hair?' asked Jack, even more curious. The description matched the red hair Jack had found at the scene.

'Yes,' said Jean Paul. 'It was very bright – just like those clowns in the circus. Unmistakable,' he muttered as his eyes drifted off into the blue sky.

'Great,' said Jack, 'you've been really helpful. I only need to do one more thing, to rule you out as a suspect. Can I take a strand of your hair?'

Jean Paul looked at him, obviously confused. 'I guess so,' he said to Jack as he pulled one of his reddish-brown hairs from his head.

Jack reached back into his Book Bag and grabbed his DNA Decoder box. Opening it, he placed Jean Paul's hair next to the one he had found in the *Mona Lisa* room and

closed it. Punching the 'match' button on the box, he waited for it to tell him whether Jean Paul's hair and the one he found were from the same person.

When the words 'NO MATCH' appeared, he turned to Jean Paul.

'Thanks for your help,' he said. 'You're no longer a suspect. I'll tell Chief Inspector Pierre that I have spoken to you. Would it be all right if we contacted you again?'

'Sure,' said Jean Paul. 'Can I go home now?'

'Sure can,' said Jack, and he waved goodbye as the man walked off.

Jack thought about what Jean Paul had said. The person who stole the painting penetrated the security of the Louvre and did it without being noticed. Most importantly, this person had a glove with a built-in laser. Very few small-time crooks had access to this kind of technology.

Jack thought it was about time to pay a visit to the owner of the company responsible for security at the Louvre and understand more about what had happened last night. He rang Chief Inspector Pierre, who told him the man in question was Denis Dupré, owner of Paris Sécurité on the Champs Elysées.

Jack consulted his map and set off with questions still buzzing in his head. He hoped that after talking to Denis Dupré things would be clearer and he'd be closer to solving the mystery of the *Mona Lisa*.

Chapter 8:
The Big Cheese

The Champs Elysées was a famous street in Paris that led down to another notable landmark, the Arc de Triomphe. Jack had seen the massive concrete arch of the Arc de Triomphe as he was running after Jean Paul. He walked up to the Paris Sécurité building and into the grand reception area.

Seated at the reception desk was a young woman with short, spiky black hair and a diamond nose ring. She was chewing gum so loudly that Jack could hear the pop and snap of every chew from the moment he entered the building.

'Hi there,' Jack said to her. 'I am here to see Denis Dupré.'

She stared at Jack for a moment and then began to blow the biggest bubble that he had ever seen. It grew until it covered her entire face, then burst with a pop into the air.

'Do you have an appointment?' she said, using her tongue to gather the deflated gum back into her mouth.

Jack wondered if she was usually this professional. 'No, but I am investigating the disappearance of the *Mona Lisa* for Chief Inspector Pierre,' said Jack. 'I am hoping he will agree to see me.'

She picked up a phone and dialled a number. 'Someone is here to see you about the *Mona Lisa*,' she said into the receiver. There was a pause. She glanced up at Jack.

'He'll see you,' she said, chewing and popping her gum again. 'Take the lift to the third floor. His office is down the hall.'

Jack did as she instructed, got out of the lift and hurried down the hallway towards Monsieur Dupré's office. It wasn't hard to find, as the office took up half of the entire floor. Jack knocked.

'What do you want?' boomed a voice from the other side.

Jack opened the large double doors and found Monsieur Dupré finishing off his lunch – an entire spit-roasted chicken on a plate. Monsieur Dupré was a burly man, almost the size of the desk he was sitting behind. His fingers were greasy from handling the chicken, and bits of his meal were smeared across his face.

'Hello there,' said Jack, careful not to extend his hand and get it covered with grease. 'I am investigating the disappearance of the *Mona Lisa*. Since your firm handles the security for the Louvre, I thought I should speak to you.'

'About what?!' Monsieur Dupré bellowed.

'Well, I would like to know more about your firm and who was working on the night of the theft,' Jack explained.

'The police have already spoken to us,' Monsieur Dupré said, snapping off a chicken wing and sending parts of his lunch splattering across the room. 'Why should I speak to *you*?'

'I am running a separate investigation on behalf of the police and would appreciate any information you could provide,' Jack answered politely. 'Chief Inspector Pierre told me you'd be helpful.' He forced a smile.

Monsieur Dupré groaned, annoyed that Jack had interrupted his lunch. 'Look, kid, we're the largest security firm in Paris. We specialize in security for some of the top museums in the city. We handle the Louvre, the Musée d'Orsay and, of course, the Pompidou. All of our security officers are well-trained and reliable. It's a pity that the *Mona Lisa* was stolen, but I can assure you we had nothing to do with it.'

'Maybe you didn't, sir,' said Jack, 'but perhaps someone who works for you knows something.'

'That's rubbish! I am Denis Dupré, owner of this firm,' he roared, raising his voice and slamming his grimy fists down on the desk, 'and I don't hire any crooks!'

Jack could tell that Monsieur Dupré was a bit sensitive – after all, by now most of the world was blaming his firm for not taking better care of the *Mona Lisa*. But Jack needed to speak to Monsieur Dupré's security officers to find out if they knew or had seen anything. He wasn't about to give up now just because the boss was having a tantrum.

'I'm not suggesting that your firm doesn't have a good reputation,' Jack said soothingly. 'It's just that it might be helpful to speak to the officer who was on duty last night.'

'He's unavailable,' bristled Monsieur Dupré. 'He was questioned so much last night that I gave him the day off.'

'Well unfortunately I still need to speak to him today,' said Jack. 'Can you ask him to call me as soon as he can? He can reach me through Chief Inspector Pierre's office. I'm sure you understand how important it is to solve this crime as quickly as possible.'

'Yes. Well, OK,' said Monsieur Dupré, settling down.

'Thanks for your time,' said Jack as he walked towards the double doors. Just as he was leaving the room, something caught his eye. A row of photographs hung on the wall and in one of them there was a man with bright red hair.

That's an odd coincidence, thought Jack. Thoughts started to pop into his head. 'Excuse me,' he said to Monsieur Dupré, pointing to the red-haired man, 'what is his name?'

'That's Carl Ponte,' said Monsieur Dupré, clearing his throat.

'Was he working at the Louvre last night?' Jack asked.

'As a matter of fact,' said Monsieur

Dupré, 'he was. He was guarding the Ancient Egypt room. Carl's an excellent security guard,' he added. 'He's newly qualified, and a specialist in surveillance. He's over at the Musée d'Orsay right now. They've asked him to take a look at their systems in light of what happened last night.'

'That's probably a good idea,' agreed Jack, starting to think that Carl's working at the Louvre last night might have been more than a coincidence. 'Thanks for your help.' He opened the doors to Monsieur Dupré's office and hurried out. *'Au revoir!'*

As Jack walked down the hall and towards the lift, he thought about what he'd learned from Denis Dupré. If Jack's hunch was right, then this security guard named Carl probably had something to do with the theft of the painting. But there was no way Jack could arrest him without solid evidence. He needed to speak to Carl first and figure out whether his theory was right.

Jack opened his map and found the location of the Musée d'Orsay. There was no time to walk. He needed a cab. He dashed through the entrance of the building and out onto the street. He lifted his arm and hailed the first taxi in sight.

'I need to get to the Musée d'Orsay – and fast!' said Jack to the taxi driver as he climbed into the car.

'*Oui!*' said the man as he slammed on the accelerator and sped down the Champs Elysées.

Chapter 9:
The Red-Haired Man

Within minutes, the taxi arrived at the front of the Musée d'Orsay, a converted train station located close to the River Seine. Jack jumped out and rushed inside. There was a group of security officers chatting in the reception area. One of them turned towards him.

'The museum's closed today, young man,' he said.

'I know,' said Jack, flashing his GPF badge. 'I am here to see one of the security officers on duty. Can you tell me where I can find Carl Ponte?' he asked.

'Sure thing,' another officer said. 'He's in the Monet room testing the surveillance equipment. Quite a famous painter, that Monet,' the man rambled on. 'We have lots of his paintings in that room. They are worth quite a bit of money, which is why Carl—'

'Nice to know,' said Jack, interrupting the man. 'Where exactly is the Monet room?' he asked.

'Top floor,' explained the guard. 'There's a lift at the back of the museum.'

Jack said a quick thank-you and hurried down the hall. He took the lift to the top floor and followed the signs to the Monet room. He rounded the corner and began to enter, but stopped short at the door. Something was moving inside.

Jack peeked round the corner. A tall man, dressed in black with flaming red hair, was standing before one of the paintings. It was a lovely picture of a field filled with red flowers. As Jack watched, he placed his hands on either side of the painting and gently lifted it off the wall, then placed it on the ground. The man looked over his shoulder to see whether anyone was coming, but didn't spot Jack. He gently wrapped the painting in brown paper.

Next, the red-haired man took a small box out of his pocket and threw it on the floor. Instantly the box grew to three times its size, large enough for the painting to fit inside. He placed the painting in the box and put a sticker on it saying: HI-TECH SECURITY EQUIPMENT. Then he climbed the ladder near the security camera and reconnected some wires.

Once he was back on the floor he reached for a walkie-talkie that was clipped to his belt.

'Philippe, it's Carl. I've finished rewiring the camera in the Monet room so it shouldn't be flickering now.'

He's planning to sneak the painting out of here under everyone's nose! Jack thought to himself.

'Stop!' commanded Jack, entering the room and flashing his badge. 'By order of the Global Protection Force, I demand that you surrender yourself and return that painting to its rightful place.'

'Yeah, right, kid,' the man sneered at Jack as he picked up the box and ran out of the room.

'Thief!' yelled Jack, dashing off to follow the man. 'Someone is trying to steal one of the Monet paintings!'

The red-haired man raced along the

corridor and down a flight of stairs. Jack
was trying his hardest to catch him. But
the man was so fast, he was getting away.

'He's heading towards the entrance!'
shouted Jack as he bolted down the stairs
and onto the ground floor. 'Stop him!' he

yelled to the guards. But they were too involved in their own conversation to register what Jack was saying. The red-haired man raced past the guards, knocking one of the men off his feet and onto the ground.

'Somebody, stop him!' yelled Jack again as he sprinted out of the door. By then the guards had understood what Jack was saying and rushed to join him.

Carl Ponte darted through the crowds outside the museum and ran into the road. Waiting for him was a white van with the words CHANNEL FERRIES written on it. The passenger door flew open and the red-haired man jumped inside. The driver slammed his foot on the accelerator and the van screeched off just as Jack reached the kerb.

Panting breathlessly, Jack looked at the van and its registration plate. The

first two numbers and letter were 82 W.
Because the van was moving so fast, Jack
couldn't see anything else.

'Channel Ferries, huh?' said one of the
officers as he caught up with Jack. 'I've
done work with them before. They're a
ferry service between Calais here in
France and Dover in England. The ferry

crosses the Channel twice a day. The next crossing,' he added, looking at his watch, 'leaves in four hours.'

'That must be what he is doing,' Jack thought aloud. 'Transporting the paintings out of the country in order to sell them. I need to be on that ferry.'

Jack tapped a few numbers on his Watch Phone. 'Chief Inspector Pierre,' he said, speaking into his wrist, 'we've had another theft. Pick me up at the Musée d'Orsay. We're going to Calais.'

Chapter 10:
The Hull

Henri came to collect Jack in an unmarked car and they sped the whole way from the museum in Paris to the port in Calais. When they arrived, they positioned themselves at the departure point, where cars and trucks drove onto the ramp and into the boat.

The ferry itself was divided into two main sections – the hull, which held the cars and trucks below, and the passenger decks, which were on the upper levels. Once the ferry left the dock, no one was allowed to be in the hull or leave the upper decks to go down to their cars.

Over a hundred cars and trucks drove past Henri and Jack, but none looked like the van from the Musée d'Orsay. As Jack was thinking that perhaps Carl wasn't planning to take the paintings by boat, he spied a white van with a lone driver. He couldn't see the driver's face, but the van clearly said CHANNEL FERRIES and the registration number started with 82 W.

'Look! There it is!' said Jack, pointing to the van. 'Let's get ourselves on this ferry.'

Henri slowly drove up the ramp and into the ferry behind the van. The huge heavy door of the ferry closed with a boom behind them. Henri parked the car close to the vehicle and turned off the engine. Everything went quiet, except for the sound of the chief inspector quickly breathing in and out in anticipation of

what was going to happen next. Jack
could feel his heart pounding too as he
saw the door of the van open and a man
climb out.

Chapter 11:
The Desperate Struggle

'It's the red-haired man!' gasped the chief inspector as he watched the thief get out of the truck. The man locked the door and made his way to the stairs leading to the passenger decks.

'All passengers must be on the upper levels in thirty minutes,' boomed a voice over the loudspeaker, 'as the ferry will depart promptly at 17:00 hours.'

'OK,' said Jack, turning to Henri. 'We have thirty minutes. Let's see what's in the van.'

Jack and Henri got out of the car and carefully walked forwards. They tried to open the back doors of the truck, but as expected they were locked.

Jack rifled through his Secret Agent Book Bag and took out his Magic Key Maker. He inserted the long rubber stick into the keyhole. Instantly, the rubber hardened to form a key. Jack turned it and the lock popped open.

Henri and Jack pulled open the doors to reveal what was inside. Jack's eyes opened wide. Inside the van were lots of objects wrapped in brown paper, just like the paper he'd seen Carl use at the Musée d'Orsay. He picked up the nearest one and handed it to Henri.

The chief inspector opened the object with trembling hands. He gasped as he looked at a small statue of a ballerina. 'It's a bronze statue by Rodin,' he said. 'It's been missing from the Rodin Museum for over two months!'

The next package was about the same size. The chief inspector unwrapped it and gasped again. 'This one is an African mask from the Musée de l'Homme. We thought this had been broken into two pieces! This must be the original and the broken pieces are a hoax!'

Jack climbed further inside and spied what looked like a painting. He peeled back the wrapper to reveal a painting of a woman in a brown dress, folding her hands over her stomach and smiling at Jack.

'Oh my!' exclaimed Henri. 'It's the *Mona Lisa*! Jack, we must be careful,' he whispered cautiously. 'The people who have stolen these pieces of artwork are very dangerous. They will probably do whatever it takes to prevent anyone from upsetting their plans.'

Suddenly Chief Inspector Pierre

snapped his head round in the direction
of the stairs leading to the upper levels.
He turned back to Jack. He looked
frightened. 'He's back! Quickly, Jack, you
must get out of the—'

THWACK! Something came down heavily
on the chief inspector's head and he
collapsed onto the floor outside the van.
The red-haired man stepped from behind
Henri with a club in his right hand.

'We meet again, kid,' he sneered. 'But this time you're really going to regret coming after me.'

Jack froze. The man gave an evil laugh and went to slam the doors closed.

'No!' cried Jack, diving towards him. But it was too late. He crashed into the doors, knocking his Watch Phone against them as they shut, trapping him inside.

Chapter 12:
The Darkness

Jack squinted his eyes and tried to see through the darkness. Thankfully, there was a little light coming from an air vent above. He looked at his Watch Phone, but it wasn't working. He must have banged it a bit too hard, he reckoned, when he crashed into the doors trying to get Carl.

Jack paused for a minute and tried to think of what to do. He thought of Max and what his brother would do in a situation like this. Since Max was taller than Jack, he figured he'd probably try to get out through the vent above.

'That's it!' Jack said to himself. Although he couldn't reach the vent from where he was, he knew he had a gadget that could help him do it. He reached into his bag and fumbled around. He took out what felt like an ordinary piece of wood, but Jack knew this was the GPF's Ratchet Step. He placed it on the floor and stood on top.

'Six steps, please,' Jack commanded. *CLICK. CLICK. CLICK.* The piece of wood built itself upwards into the form of a ladder. It was just high enough to lift Jack up to the hole.

Unfortunately he was too big to fit through, but Jack had another idea. He ejected his Melting Ink Pen from the side of his Watch Phone and placed it on the ceiling of the van. He drew a circle around the vent. The ink from the pen melted through the steel and Jack quietly pulled

himself out of the van and onto the roof.

He looked out across the hull and towards the back of the van. He could see Chief Inspector Pierre unconscious on the floor with the club lying beside him, but there was no sign of the red-haired man. Although his watch didn't work, Jack figured he had about fifteen minutes before the ferry departed. Frustratingly, he wasn't even close to capturing Carl.

Jack carefully climbed down the back of the truck and knelt down beside Henri. He reached into his pocket and pulled out a small tub of Time-Release Vapours, then rubbed some under Henri's nose.

'That should help you to wake up shortly,' whispered Jack. Just then, he heard the red-haired man's voice coming from the front of the van.

'Yeah, the kid is here,' Carl said. 'I've got him in the back of the van. Not sure what I am going to do with him and the inspector. I don't really want anyone else from the GPF on our tail. Any suggestions, boss?'

Boss, thought Jack. So there is someone else behind this.

'Right, no problem,' continued Carl. 'I'll get rid of them. I'll toss them into the sea during the voyage. Speak to you when I reach Dover.'

Jack heard the beep as Carl hung up. Then he seemed to be fumbling for something in the front seat of the van. Jack had to act quickly, or he and Henri were toast.

Jack climbed back onto the top of the van. He saw Carl open the front door and step out with a rope in his hands. The thief made his way towards the back of the truck and the chief inspector.

Carl knelt down beside Henri, who was still unconscious, and snapped the rope tight between his two hands. Just as Carl was about to wrap the rope around his neck, Henri's eyes opened. The Time-Release Vapours had worked!

'Get off me, you thief!' Henri shouted at the red-haired man. The chief inspector grabbed the rope and struggled with the man for control. With one swift move, Carl grabbed his club and whacked Henri on the head again, knocking him unconscious for a second time.

Chapter 13:
The Deadly Glove

'Leave him alone!' screamed Jack from
above as he jumped onto the man's back.

Carl Ponte stood up quickly, throwing
Jack off his back and onto the floor. 'That
will teach you, you little brat!' He scowled.

From the back pocket of his trousers,
Carl pulled out a black glove and put it on
his right hand. Out of his fingertips shot
five red lasers. He aimed the glove in
Jack's direction.

Quickly, Jack dived between two cars.
ZAP! The lasers sliced through the front

end of one of the cars.

'Come here, kid. Let me show you how this laser really works,' Carl sniggered. Jack scurried between the cars.

'You can't get away from me, you little punk,' he said, now running in Jack's direction.

Jack could hear the whirr of the laser coming closer. He hurried down the lane of vehicles and hid behind a red truck.

'You can't hide for ever,' the man growled.

Jack rummaged desperately through his Book Bag. 'Where is it? Where is it!?' he muttered to himself. He was searching for the one thing that might be able to save him. 'That's it!' he said aloud as he pulled the life-saving gadget out of his bag. He took a deep breath and stood up from behind the red truck. He looked directly at the red-haired man.

'OK, Carl!' Jack yelled. 'Give me all you've got!'

Chapter 14:
The Hypno-Disc

The red-haired man lifted his glove and aimed the razor-sharp lasers at Jack. Instantly, Jack lifted his left hand. In it was a round, flat disc with swirls of colour.

Jack was holding the mother of all secret-agent gadgets: the Hypno-Disc. Normally, the Hypno-Disc would spin in a clockwise direction, throwing out a light that, when seen, would hypnotize someone on the spot. But Jack had activated the reverse mechanism. Instead of sending out light, the Hypno-Disc was sucking in all the light from Carl's deadly laser glove, making it useless.

Carl stood facing Jack with a look of panic on his face. The red-haired man had failed in his attempt to kill Jack, and now Jack had all the power.

The evil villain looked closely at the Hypno-Disc. He had never seen one before, but he had heard about its powers. The red-haired man gulped and did what any sensible criminal would do: he dropped to the floor and began pleading for mercy.

'Please don't hurt me, kid,' Carl begged. 'I didn't mean it. I was just doing what I was told to do.'

Jack thought for a moment. He would never kill Carl, but it didn't hurt to make him squirm. 'I suppose I could spare your life,' he said, 'if you tell me who you are working for and why you've been stealing

these important pieces of art.'

Just then, Jack heard a noise from behind Carl's van.

'Oh, my head!' groaned the voice. 'What happened?' It was Chief Inspector Pierre. He pulled himself up and looked around. 'Are you OK, Jack?' he called over.

'Sure am, Chief Inspector,' replied Jack.

Henri ambled over to join Jack, rubbing the bump on his head.

'It was my boss, Denis Dupré, who made me do this,' confessed Carl, sobbing into his hands. 'He told me that if I helped him steal these precious pieces of art, he would give me one million euros so that I could repay my debts. He was planning to sell them to private collectors living in other countries—'

'But surely,' interrupted Chief Inspector

Pierre, 'someone would have seen these works and arrested the people who bought them.'

'These works of art were for very special private collections,' explained Carl, 'so no one but the owners would have seen them.'

'How were you able to steal the *Mona Lisa* without anyone knowing?' asked Jack.

'Monsieur Dupré had it arranged that the guard on duty would turn off the surveillance equipment between 7:50 and 7:55 p.m.,' explained Carl. 'That way, I could steal the painting and there would be no record of my entering or exiting the room.' Carl looked pleadingly at Henri and Jack.

'Well,' said Jack to Henri, 'what should we do with him?'

Chief Inspector Pierre walked behind Carl. He grabbed Carl's wrists and held them behind his back. Out of his pocket he pulled a pair of handcuffs. He clamped them onto Carl's wrists and dragged him into a standing position.

'For now,' said the chief inspector, looking at his watch, 'I think we should get off this boat and hand him to the port authorities. We have bigger fish to fry,' he added. 'Denis Dupré is responsible for this. I think it's time we paid him a visit together.'

Chapter 15:
The Big Cheese
Revisited

Jack and the chief inspector walked into
the glass atrium of the Paris Sécurité
office on the Champs Elysées. They
marched past the woman at the front
desk, who was busily reading a book and
chewing away at her gum. By the time she
had noticed them they had already
entered the lift and were on their way up
to the third floor.

Jack and Henri walked down the hallway
towards Monsieur Dupré's office. Without
knocking, Chief Inspector Pierre flung

open the door. Monsieur Dupré was sitting at his desk with his back facing Jack and Henri. He was so engrossed in a phone conversation that he didn't even hear them enter the room.

'Yes, that's right,' said Monsieur Dupré into the receiver. 'You can have the actual *Mona Lisa* by that artist Da . . . Da . . . Da . . . Yeah, that's the one . . . for the reasonable price of one hundred million euros.'

'Ahem!' coughed Henri, in an attempt to get Monsieur Dupré's attention.

'Huh?' said Monsiuer Dupré as he looked over his shoulder. When he saw that it was Jack and the chief inspector, he spun his chair round so fast that he banged his knee on the corner of the desk. 'Owwww!' he howled in pain. Hunched over the desk and rubbing his knee, he slowly put the receiver down.

'I arrest you, Denis Dupré, for masterminding the theft of the *Mona Lisa* and the other works of art found in Carl Ponte's possession,' declared Chief Inspector Pierre as he walked behind the desk to handcuff Denis.

'What? This is ridiculous!' shouted Monsieur Dupré, standing up in protest. 'I am Denis Dupré, owner of this firm, and I had nothing to do with anything! That phone call,' he said, trying to explain

what Jack and Henri had overheard, 'I . . .
I . . . I . . . was just pretending. I don't
know anything about the *Mona Lisa*!'

'That's not what your accomplice, Carl
Ponte, said,' remarked Henri as he placed
the handcuffs on the man's wrists. 'He
has identified you as the mastermind
behind the operation. And I believe him.'
Chief Inspector Pierre pulled Monsieur
Dupré from behind his desk and over to
Jack.

'This is because of you, isn't it?' growled Denis angrily at Jack.

'Yep,' said Jack, 'and I hope that you have learned your lesson. You should never take something that doesn't belong to you.'

'You little—' The big man turned red with rage as he lunged towards him.

'Thanks, Jack,' said Henri, holding out his hand to shake Jack's. 'We couldn't have done this without you. The city of Paris is especially grateful.'

'No problem,' said Jack. 'I'm glad that I was able to help. You know where to find me if you need me again,' he offered.

'Let's hope we don't,' replied Henri, 'but you know you're welcome in France anytime.'

Jack smiled at him and tried to avoid the evil glares from Monsieur Dupré.

'Now, let's see if we can find a comfortable cell for you to spend a nice long holiday in,' the chief inspector said to Denis as he led him down the hall.

Henri waved to Jack as he and Monsieur Dupré stepped into the lift. Jack waved back.

Chapter 16:
The Lift Home

Well, I guess it's time for me to get home, Jack thought to himself.

He walked over to the second lift and pushed the down button. The doors sprang open and Jack stepped inside. Out of his Book Bag he pulled a round button with the letter H on it and placed it over the G for ground floor. He pushed it and the button began to glow.

'Home, please,' said Jack to the button, and the lift began to move downwards. As it descended, he yelled, 'Off to England!'

When the lift doors opened again, Jack found himself in the middle of his bedroom, just as he had left it. As he stepped out of the lift it vanished behind him. He walked over to his clock and looked at the time: 7:31 p.m. Perfect, he thought as he walked over to his desk. He picked up the unfinished drawing of his comic-book hero, Super Smash, and sat down.

'Now,' said Jack, 'it's time to finish him off.'

Jack lifted his pencil and began to draw. He knew his sketch would never be as famous as some of the works of art he saw in Paris. But he didn't care. Art, after all, Jack reckoned, wasn't about fame, it was about fun. And that's just what Jack was doing now – having a blast drawing Super Smash destroying Tortua with a powerful disc that stole her power. Now that, thought Jack, is a great idea.

Turn to the
next page and
read the first
two chapters of
The Secret of
the Sacred
Temple . . .

The Secret of the
Sacred Temple:
CAMBODIA

Read the first two
chapters here

Chapter 1:
The Annoying One

'And then you'll never guess what happened,' gushed Lily, Jack's eleven-year-old cousin. She was visiting Jack's family from Devon, where Jack's Aunt Emma, Lily's mum, lived. 'My friend Luke stood in front of the class to read his essay and didn't even know that his shirt-tail was stuck in the zip of his trousers! Isn't that embarrassing?'

The whole family – Jack, his dad, his mum and Lily – were sitting around the dinner table finishing a delicious fish-and-chip supper. If the story had been told by anyone else, Jack would have found it funny. But because it was told by his annoying cousin, he just rolled his eyes and looked at his mum.

'That's a nice story, Lily,' said Jack's mum to Lily. 'Did anything exciting happen to you today?' she asked, turning her attention to Jack.

Just as Jack was about to tell his family about how he had scored a corker of a goal in today's football match, he spied the clock hanging on the wall above his mother's head. It read 7:28 p.m. He looked back at his mum and smiled before he leaped from his chair and headed for the kitchen door.

'Lots of stuff, Mum,' said Jack, 'but it'll have to wait until tomorrow. I've got maths homework to do!' He left the kitchen and quickly climbed the stairs to his bedroom.

Jack's dad, who had up until now listened silently to the conversation at the table, said proudly, 'It's wonderful that Jack has taken such an interest in maths.'

As Jack began to open his bedroom door, he could hear his cousin talking again downstairs. 'Guess what happened to my friend Frieda McCauley today?' she squealed excitedly to her aunt and uncle.

'Someone stole a hairbrush out of her bag!'

Poor Mum and Dad, Jack thought, shaking his head. Glad I have some maths homework. He smiled to himself as he opened the door and stepped into his top-secret bedroom.

Chapter 2:
The Secret

Jack entered the room, hung his 'KEEP OUT'
sign on the doorknob and closed the
door behind him. There was always the
possibility that a family member would
walk in and discover something Jack
didn't want them to see – like Whizzy
telling him about his next mission, or Jack
surveying his latest hi-tech gadgets.

Jack was a secret agent for the Global
Protection Force. The Global Protection
Force, or GPF, sent Jack around the globe
in order to protect the world's most
precious people, places and things.

'*Protect that which cannot protect itself*' was the motto of the Global Protection Force. The organization was started in 1947 by a man named Ronald Barter who decided he'd had enough of crooks trying to destroy things that mattered in the world. Things like beautiful pieces of art, endangered animals, famous buildings, or even famous people who were trying to do something positive. When he died in 1962 (in mysterious circumstances), his son Gerald took over and made the GPF one of the leading worldwide forces against crime.

Jack joined the GPF after his older brother, Max, disappeared. Although no one else in his family knew that Max was a secret agent for the GPF, Jack did. That was because Max had told him.

Max used to show Jack his secret-agent gadgets and explain how they worked as he told him stories about using each one on his missions. Jack looked forward to those times with Max so he could hear all about the adventures. Although lots of brothers their age didn't get on, Jack and Max got on well. They were more like best friends.

Then Max was sent by the GPF to a supposed school in Switzerland.

When Jack received the anonymous note telling him his brother was in danger, he quickly signed up to join the GPF and dedicated his life to finding Max. As soon as he was on the 'inside', he asked the GPF about Max's whereabouts, but the GPF wouldn't tell Jack a thing. They denied any involvement in Max's disappearance and immediately sealed Max's files.

Even so, Jack always hoped that one of his missions would lead to some information about Max. Who knows? thought Jack that evening, maybe this mission will be the one.

SECRET-AGENT NOTES

SECRET-AGENT NOTES

SECRET-AGENT NOTES